HAMLET
AND THE MAGNIFICENT SANDCASTLE

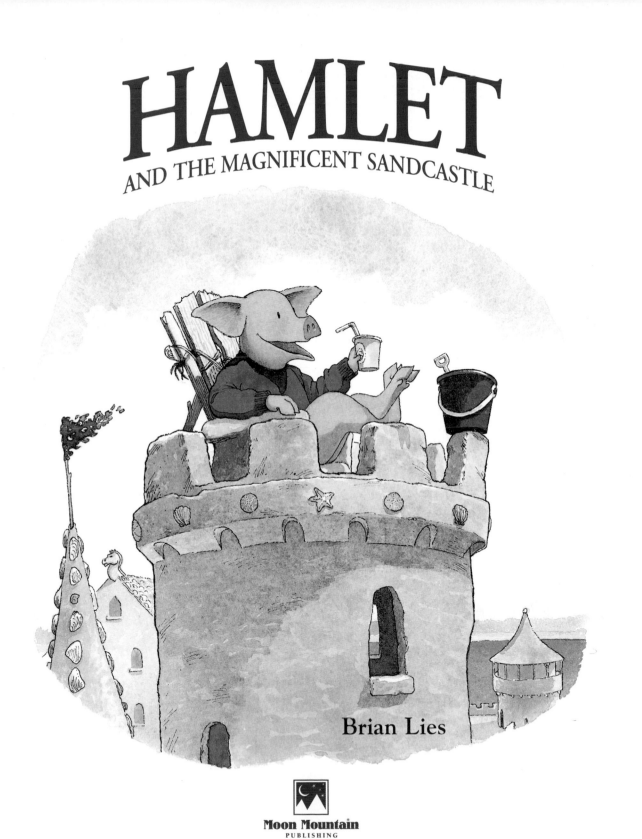

Brian Lies

Moon Mountain
PUBLISHING

North Kingstown, Rhode Island

Text and Illustrations Copyright © 2001 Brian Lies

First Edition.

Publisher's Cataloging-in-Publication
Lies, Brian.
    Hamlet and the magnificent sandcastle / by Brian Lies. -- 1st ed.
    p. cm.
    SUMMARY: Hamlet, a pig with a vision, determines to build the
biggest sandcastle in the world. His porcupine friend Quince is his
reluctant partner who worries that things will go wrong. And sure
enough, when the tide comes in it brings trouble.
    Audience: Ages 5-8.
    LCCN 00-110943
    ISBN 0-9677929-2-4

    1. Sandcastles--Juvenile fiction. 2. Pigs--Juvenile fiction.
3. Porcupines--Juvenile fiction. I. Title.

PZ7.L618Haml 2001   [E]
             QBI00-901967

Moon Mountain Publishing
80 Peachtree Road
North Kingstown, RI 02852
www.moonmountainpub.com

The illustrations in this book were done in watercolor on Arches hot
press paper.

Printed in South Korea

10 9 8 7 6 5 4 3 2 1

For Sam Keith—
author and adventurer

"It'll be great!" Hamlet said, as he tucked his bucket and shovel under the train seat. "I'm going to build the biggest sandcastle in the whole world!"

"I still think it's a terrible idea," Quince grumbled. "Like the time you tried to build your own skis. You remember how that turned out!" He waved his paws in the air, and Hamlet leaned away. It's never a good idea to get too close to a worried porcupine, even if he is your best friend.

"What about splinters from driftwood?" Quince continued. "You might be bitten by a crab. Or stung by a jellyfish!"

Hamlet rolled his eyes. "I'll be fine! After all, you're here to make sure nothing goes wrong."

But Quince was always worried about something. "And what about sharks? Or quicksand?" he added.

"Have you ever seen quicksand at the beach?" Hamlet laughed.

"No...but that doesn't mean it's not there!"

Hamlet gazed out the window and daydreamed as the train rumbled toward the shore. The wheels on the track clacked a rhythm that sounded like "Castle—castle—castle."

Quince heard the wheels too, but he heard "Careful—careful—careful!"

When they got to the beach, it was completely empty. Hamlet felt like laughing and yelling at the same time. A brisk breeze blew off the ocean, the sun shone brightly, and miles and miles of perfect, buildable sand stretched out in both directions. Hamlet ran toward the ocean and started to dig.

"Don't you think you're too close to the water?" Quince called. "The tide will wreck your castle."

Hamlet shook his head. "We'll be on our way home long before then!"

But Quince wasn't convinced. He unfolded his beach chair and raised the umbrella. "I'll set up right here, where I can watch you," he announced. He slathered himself with sunscreen, pulled a clock from his bag and set it down next to him. They weren't going to miss the train home—not if he could help it. Quince shook his head grimly. "Trouble! Trouble's coming! I can smell it!"

"You smell low tide," Hamlet called back, laughing.

Hamlet hauled bucket after bucket of sand to his growing castle. In the center he built a Great Hall, with massive towers around its edges. Battlements, buttresses and arches soared into the sky, and flags of seaweed sprouted proudly from the highest points, snapping in the wind.

Quince watched carefully, trying to spot quicksand, jellyfish and sharp driftwood, but the warm sun and soft crashing of the waves were too peaceful. He struggled to keep his eyes open. "Hamlet will get into trouble unless I'm watching!" he thought. Within minutes he was fast asleep.

The sandcastle grew bigger and bigger. Hamlet dug a deep moat and carved out tunnels, winding stairways and a secret passage. He made an underground dungeon with driftwood bars on the door, and built a treasure room, a kitchen and stables. He carved suits of armor, and crafted banners and tapestries from seaweed.

Back in his beach chair, Quince awoke with a startled yelp. He'd been soaked by a wave. Rising water surrounded him, the sky had turned gray and angry, and his clock was nowhere to be seen. It was clear he'd been asleep too long. With a wail, he grabbed his gear and splashed toward the castle to warn Hamlet. He barely made it to the entrance through the quickly rising tide.

Hamlet was working on a banquet table for the Great Hall when he heard the scratchy sound of running paws. Quince appeared in the archway, looking frightened and wet.

"I fell asleep, Hamlet!" he squeaked. "I was supposed to be watching, and I fell asleep! We're doomed!"

Hamlet grinned. "I'm not doomed. I'm having fun. Just look at this place!"

"You don't understand, Hamlet. There's water everywhere!"

"Of course there is," Hamlet said. "We're at the beach!"

He glanced out a window—and dropped his shovel. Everything looked different. The beach was gone, and in its place was a vast, churning sea. *Where had the time gone?*

"We'll be all right," he said, trying to sound confident. "See? These walls are six feet thick. We'll be fine!"

"I don't know about that, Hamlet," Quince said. The rising waves made dry ground—and safety—seem far away.

Then they felt a heavy, muffled THUD. Hamlet sprinted off down a hallway. Quince ran after him, and shrieked when he saw the toppled ruins of the East Wing, with open, angry ocean gnawing at its edges.

Hamlet drooped. "The dungeon and my tapestries were in there," he moaned. "Let's go to the Great Tower. That's really solid."

They hurried up the stairs to the top of the tower. Hamlet peered over the edge and groaned as one part of the castle after another plunged into the dark, roiling water. Splash! "There go the western battlements," he mourned. Splash! "And the stables..." Splash! Splash! "Darn! I thought for sure the Great Hall would be OK!"

Quince couldn't watch. He curled up in the center of the tower and squeaked, "I knew this was a bad idea! I knew there'd be trouble! I knew it! I knew it! I knew it!"

"We'll be OK, Quince. We'll just wait here until the tide goes out again," Hamlet said nervously. "We could always swim for it if we had to."

"I can't!" Quince wailed. "I don't know how to swim!"

Hamlet paled. "You don't? I didn't know that!" That changed everything.

Before Hamlet could begin to think of a way out, an evil-looking crack snaked across the middle of the floor. There was a shifting, grinding sound, and half of the tower plummeted into the water.

"Now what do we do?" Hamlet yelled in desperation.

"I know!" Quince squeaked. "My umbrella!" He wrestled it open, turned it upside down, and jumped in.

"A boat!" Hamlet cried. He leaped into it. In that split second, the last of the tower fell from beneath them and plunged into the ocean. There was a sickening drop, a jarring splash, and then...they were floating.

Hamlet whooped with relief. "It worked! What a great idea, Quince! Sandcastles and boating, all in the same day!"

But Quince wasn't cheering. "Um...I've got more bad news..."

"What?" Hamlet asked sharply. Quince's voice scared him.

"My quills. I punctured the umbrella when we got in. We're sinking!"

Hamlet's stomach fell. "We...we won't sink," he quavered. "We're too close to shore."

Quince shook his head. "We're not going that way."

He was right. Hamlet could feel a strong current pulling them out to sea. He groaned. "If only we had a paddle, or a motor or something."

Quince sat up. "But we do have a sail, sort of. What about my beach chair?"

"That's it!" Hamlet cried, grabbing the chair. "Perfect!"

They tied it to the handle of the umbrella, and the canvas of the chair made a sharp cracking sound as it filled with wind.

The umbrella began to surge forward, and Hamlet struggled to hold the beach chair straight. Towering, choppy waves rose and fell under them. Quince bailed desperately as icy water slopped over the umbrella's sides and streamed through the holes his quills had made.

It seemed like they'd never reach the shore. Quince had to stop bailing every few minutes to catch his breath. And when he did, the water rose so fast he had to bail even faster just to catch up. Hamlet was starting to lose hope when the umbrella ground to a sudden stop a few yards from shore.

Quince pitched himself over the side and dashed onto the beach, soaked and sputtering. Hamlet followed, dragging the umbrella behind him.

"I'm soaked! Drenched! Waterlogged!" Quince wailed. "We'll catch cold. Or pneumonia! And it's all my fault!"

"It's not your fault," Hamlet sighed. "I wasn't paying attention—"

"I was supposed to be paying attention, and I fell asleep. It *is* my fault," Quince insisted. He felt terrible.

They trudged back to the train station. When the train arrived, they dropped into their seats, cold and miserable.

Someone walked by carrying a hot drink and Hamlet raised an eyebrow. He knew what they needed. Without saying a word, he went to the cafe car and came back carrying two steaming cups of hot chocolate, heaped with marshmallows. Quince's eyes brightened. They sipped the hot chocolate, and its warmth made them feel better.

"I'm sorry your sandcastle got wrecked," Quince said. "It really was the best one I've ever seen."

"I should have built it stronger," Hamlet sighed. "But thanks." He thought about all the things he hadn't had a chance to finish. *Next time,* he vowed.

Hamlet knew that Quince still blamed himself. "The boat and the sail were terrific," he said. "We'd still be out there if you hadn't thought of them."

Quince started to grin. He really *had* helped, hadn't he?

"Hey, Quince!" Hamlet said, sitting up straight. "Speaking of adventures—I just had a great idea!"

Quince saw Hamlet's face, and his stomach sank. He knew that look, and it meant *trouble*.

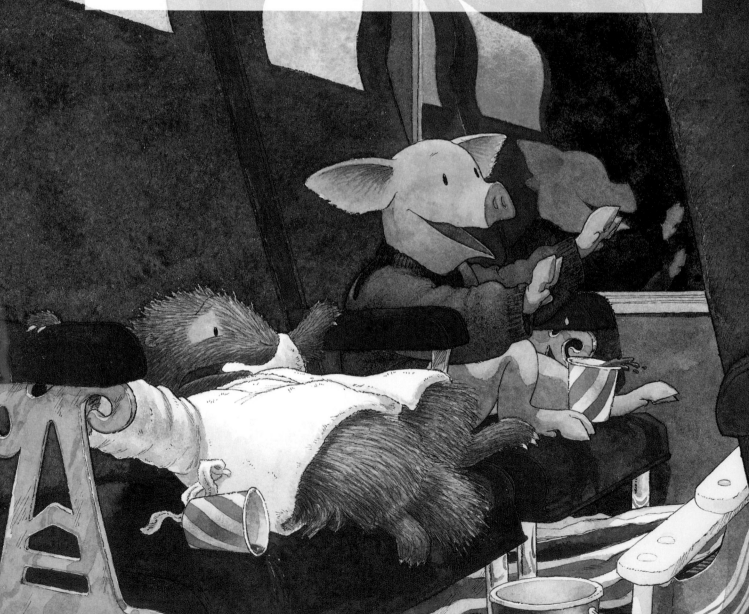